Andy Griffith[...] [...]azing
treehouse with [...] [...]riend Terry and
together they make funny books, just
like the one you're holding in your hands
right now. Andy writes the words and
Terry draws the pictures. If you'd like to
know more, read the Treehouse series
(or visit www.andygriffiths.com.au).

Terry Denton lives in an amazing
treehouse with his friend Andy and
together they make funny books, just
like the one you're holding in your hands
right now. Terry draws the pictures and
Andy writes the words. If you'd like to
know more, read the Treehouse series
(or visit www.terrydenton.com).

Jill Griffiths lives near Andy and Terry
in a house full of animals. She has
two dogs, one goat, three horses, four
goldfish, one cow, two guinea pigs,
one camel, one donkey, one cat, one
frogpotamous, three snakes and so many
rabbits she has lost count. If you'd like to
know more, read the Treehouse series.

Climb higher every time
with the Treehouse series

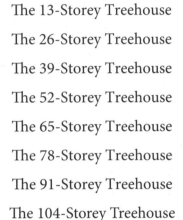

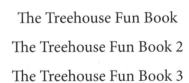

THE TREEHOUSE FUN BOOK 3

JILL GRIFFITHS
ANDY GRIFFITHS
and TERRY DENTON

MACMILLAN CHILDREN'S BOOKS

First published 2018 in Pan by Pan Macmillan Australia Pty Ltd

First published in the UK 2018 by Macmillan Children's Books
an imprint of Pan Macmillan
20 New Wharf Road, London N1 9RR
Associated companies throughout the world
www.panmacmillan.com

ISBN 978-1-5098-8530-5

Text copyright © Flying Beetroot Pty Ltd 2018
Illustrations copyright © Terry Denton 2018

The right of Jill Griffiths, Andy Griffiths and Terry Denton to be identified as the
authors and illustrator of this work has been asserted by them in
accordance with the Copyright, Designs and Patents Act 1988.

1 3 5 7 9 8 6 4 2

A CIP catalogue record for this book is available from the British Library.

Typeset in 11/11.5 Drawzing by Seymour Designs
Printed in China

I'm a rabbit and I like balloons.

I'm Terry. I live in a treehouse with my friend Andy and we make books together. I draw the pictures and Andy writes the words.

pencil →

Terry →

And I'm Jill. I live in a house full of animals in the forest near my friends Andy and Terry. I like animals and solving problems and doing puzzles.

And I'm Silky.

I'm a catnary and I can fly.

And I'm Jill's favourite pet.

COME ON UP

Choose one of the things down there and draw yourself using it to get up to the treehouse.

rocket

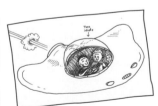

flying fried-egg car

jet-propelled swivel chair

flying beetroot

flying cat sleigh

PLAN YOUR TREEHOUSE VISIT

 There is a lot of fun stuff to do in our treehouse, like these 13 things. What order—from 1 to 13—would you do them in? Put a number in each box.

6 car-washing

3 floating

12 plate-spinning

1 combining

5 scribbling

4 ball sports

7 shark-feeding

2 enlarging

10 writing

9 drawing

8 popcorn-popping

12 whirling

11 golfing

7

TV SHOW FUN

My favourite TV show is *The Barky the Barking Dog Show*. My second favourite is *The Buzzy the Buzzing Fly Show*.

She's just so buzzy!

Can you think up some other TV shows you think I might like?

Flappy the Flapping Bird?

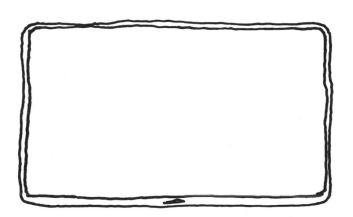

 Kooky the Crazy Cube?

 Miss Hissy the Hissing Snake?

WHO AM I?

Can you tell who these characters are? Write their names in the white spaces.

I hereby un-invent you!

Profesor Stupido

Do you have a permit for that?

Inspector Bubbl wrap

I know all and see all.

Madame Know-it-a

Mel gibbon

Mr. big shot

Bill the postman

Answers are on page 148.

11

FILL IN THE BLANKS

Can you fill in the blanks?
The answer to each one is
a level in the treehouse.

Can you tell me the level?

Can you fill in the blank?

It's home to three fish—

It's the killer shark _tank_

If you don't like going

Around and around

Then stay off the

Not-very-merry-go- _round_

I don't know any of these. I'm just a peanut.

Relax. Answers are on page 149.

The person in charge

Is a bit of a clown

It's full of his clones

And it's called <u>terrytown</u>

HAZARD

If you dare to go in

You will have entered your tomb

For there is no escape

From the treehouse Maze of <u>doom</u>

CERTAIN DEATH AHEAD.

SPOT THE DIFFERENCE

 One of these pictures of Professor Stupido is slightly different. Can you tell which one it is? Circle the number of the odd one out.

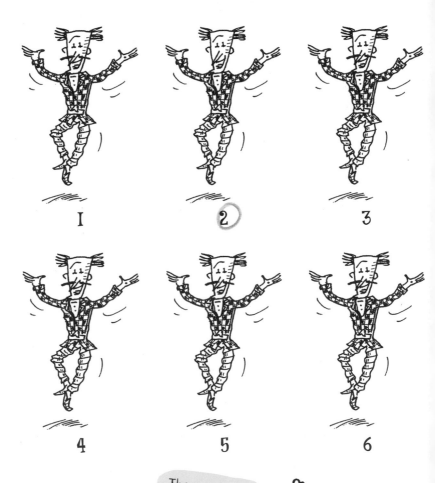

1

2

3

4

5

6

The answer is on page 150.

TREEHOUSE TRUE OR FALSE?

Tick the boxes to show if these statements are true or false.

Answers are on page 151.

T F

1. Andy painted Silky yellow to make her a catnary.

2. Captain Woodenhead is a police captain.

3. Terry is a really good drawer.

4. Andy is also a really good drawer.

5. Professor Stupido is an inventor.

6. Terry is allergic to magic beans.

7. Mel Gibbon is a monkey.

8. Andy is very good at maths.

9. Terry and Andy have a desert island level.

10. Mr Big Nose likes opera.

11. Vegetable Patty is a revenge-atarian.

12. I have an early learning centre for aliens.

13. Terry invented the spooncil.

15

RHYME TIME

Can you finish these rhymes?

Roses are red

Violets are blue

To solve a mystery

You need a C L U e

Roses are red

Violets are blue

You can pat a baby dinosaur

At the baby-dinosaur petting ZOO

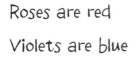

Answers are on page 152.

Roses are _red_

Violets are blue

Pets visit Jill's pet salon

When they want a new _hairdo_

Roses are red

Violets are _blue_

The number after one

Is the number _two_

PICTURE CROSSWORD

Fill in the blank crossword on the opposite page by writing the first letter of each thing pictured in the crossword below. For example, in box 1 there is a picture of a caterpillar so the letter is C.

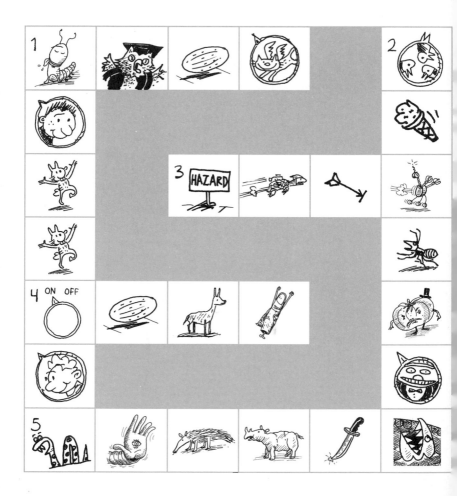

18

	1 C	O	W	S		2 P
	a					i
	r		3 S	t	a	r
	r					a
	4 O	w	l	s		t
	t					e
	5 S	h	a	r	k	s

JILL'S NUMBER QUIZ

 All the answers to these questions are numbers. How many can you answer?

What is 395x527?

208165

WOW! You're good!

1. How many storeys do Andy and Terry add to their treehouse each time?

    13

2. How many wise owls live in the treehouse?

    3

3. How many children do Andy and Terry babysit in *The 91-Storey Treehouse?*

    3

4. How many unlucky pirates were there in *The 26-Storey Treehouse?*

    10

5. How many sharks do Andy and Terry have?

   3

6. How many flavours of ice-cream in Edward Scooperhand's ice-cream parlour?

   78

7. How many grumpy old tomatoes did the really hungry caterpillar eat in *The 52-Storey Treehouse*?

   1

8. How many years did it take Terry's Ninja snails to get to Mr Big Nose's office in *The 52-Storey Treehouse*?

   100 (and 15 minutes)

9. How many flying cats fought the giant gorilla in *The 13-Storey Treehouse?*

13

10. How many plates on the plate-spinning level?

78

11. How many punches does it take The Trunkinator to knock someone out?

1

12. How many friends did Terry have before he met Andy?

0

13. How many numbers did Andy and Terry count down before blasting off in their dot-to-dot rocket in *The 39-Storey Treehouse?*

10

Answers are on page 154.

COLOUR IN BANARNIA

BUTTON-PUSHING TIME

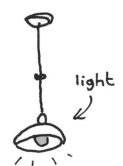

DRAW A CROWN

DRAW SCOOPER HANDS

Edward Scooperhands is missing four of his scooper arms. Can you draw them back for him? (Don't forget to draw a scoop of your favourite ice-cream in each of his scooper hands.)

HOT

91-STOREY TREEHOUSE WORD SEARCH

When you've finished there should be 13 letters left over that spell out something to do with The 91-Storey Treehouse.

WORD LIST

BABY
BABYSIT
BANARNIA
GENIE
ICE-CREAM
MEDAL
NOSE
OPERA
POSTMAN
RAINBOWS
SANDWICH
SUBMARINE
TURBAN
WEB
WHIRLPOOL

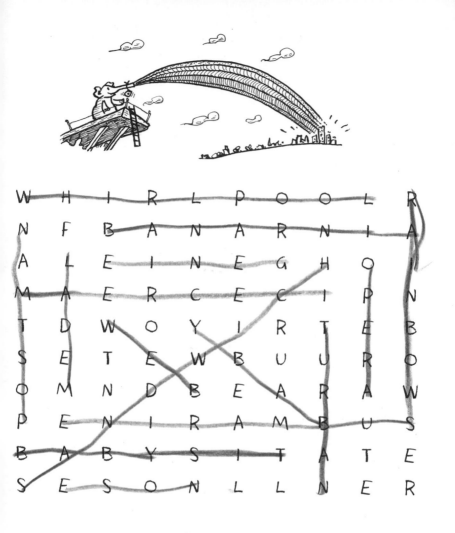

```
W H I R L P O O L R
N F B A N A R N I A
A L E I N E G H O I
M A E R C E C I P N
T D W O Y I R T E B
S E T E W B U U R O
O M N D B E A R A W
P E N I R A M B U S
B A B Y S I T A T E
S E S O N L L N E R
```

SOLUTION: Fortune teller

I can see the answer. It's on page 155.

29

FILL IN THE BLANKS

Can you finish these words?
They are all things or people
from *The 91-Storey Treehouse.*

1. SuBmarine sandwich

2. big red button

3. garbage PumP

4. tele Phone

RING RING!
RING RING!
RING RING!

5. Bill the Postman

6. crystal ball

7. _warning_ poster

8. _madam_ know-it-all

9. spin-and-win prize _wheel_

10. emergency self-inflating
underpants

11. Alice, Albert and the _baby_

12. Mr Big _nose_

Answers are on page 156.

DEFINITION QUIZ

Tick the box that has the definition that matches the word.

TRUNKINATOR

☐ one of Terry's inventions

☑ a boxing elephant

☐ a high-tech tree

☐ a robot that carries trunks

REVENGE-ATARIAN

☐ someone who eats vegetables

☐ someone who eats foods they hate

☐ someone who eats things they are allergic to

☑ someone who eats vegetables to get revenge on them

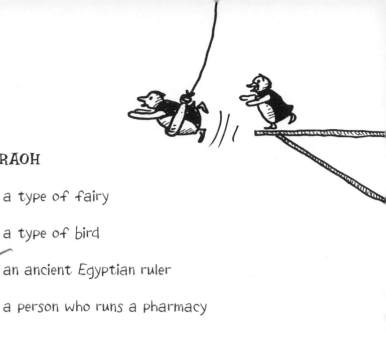

PHARAOH

- [ ] a type of fairy
- [ ] a type of bird
- [x] an ancient *Egyptian* ruler
- [ ] a person who runs a pharmacy

AUTOBIOGRAPHY

- [ ] a book written by the Once-upon-a-time machine
- [x] a person's account of his or her own life
- [ ] any book written by me (Andy)
- [ ] a motorised book

Answers are on page 156.

TREEHOUSE SUDOKU

Complete the sudoku by drawing Andy, Terry, me and Silky in the empty spaces.

HOW TO DO SUDOKU

Each picture should appear only once in each row and each column. For example:

→ ↓

Each picture should appear only once in each small square (the squares divided up by the thicker lines). For example, this square:

→

Could look like this: →

Rows go across.

Columns go down.

			terry
silky		Jill	andy
	silky		Jill
Jill	andy	terry	

HINT: start with the row or square that is almost filled in and see who's missing.

The answer is on page 157.

35

SOUND EFFECTS SUDOKU

Finish this one by writing BLAP! BLAM! BLING! and BLOOF! in the empty spaces.

Bloof	Bling	**BLAM!**	Blap
BLAP!	Blam	**BLING!**	Bloof
Bling	**BLAP!**	BLOOF!	Blam
BLAM!	BLOOF!	Blap	**BLING!**

The answer is on page 158. QUACK!

TERRY'S DRAWINGS SUDOKU

Draw a banana, a worm, a knife or a finger in each empty space.

Yum!

banana	worm	knife	finger
knife	finger	worm	Banana
finger	knife	Banana	worm
worm	banana	finger	knife

The answer is on page 159.

?

37

SMOKE SIGNAL TIME

Drawing pictures in smoke is fun.

 But don't just take my word for it. You try some. You can draw whatever you like, or you could follow the suggestions.

Butterflies are nice. Hint, hint.

 Draw a spider.

Draw a bird.

Draw a cat.

 And a horse as well.

Draw us!

MAKE A WISH

Congratulations! You now have three wishes. What would you like to wish for?

I wish ——————

I wish ——————

I wish ——————

41

OPERA TIME

Can you trace the path of Mr Big Nose's song through the word grid? Start at the letter O at the top and move up, down, backwards or forwards, but not diagonally, through the letters. I've done the first few to get you started.

OH MY BIG NOSE-IO
THE CROSSER I GET-IO
THE BIGGER IT GROWS-IO
THEN IT BOOM, CRASH, EXPLODES-IO.

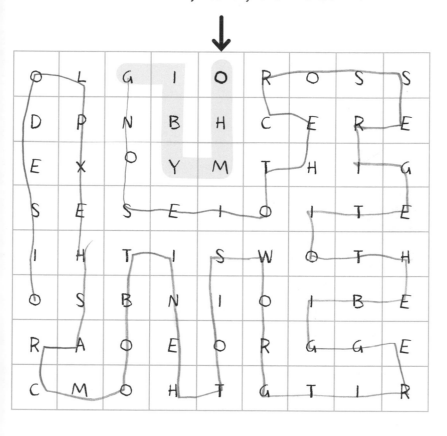

The answer is on page 160.

TRA-LAAAA!

SHADOW PUZZLE

 Which shadow matches the picture of me in the middle? Circle the number of the one that matches exactly.

1

2

3

4

The answer is on page 161.

SHADOW PUZZLE

Which shadow matches the picture of Andy in the middle? Circle the number of the one that matches him exactly.

1

2

3

4

The answer is on page 161.

I REALLY, REALLY WANT TO KNOW

These are just some of the many things Madam Know-it-all really really wants to know.

I want to know who made the colours
And gave each one a name.
And who the heck made spiders?
Is there someone we can blame?

I want to know why flowers grow,
Why rivers flow and noses blow.
I want to know where rainbows go.
I really, really want to know!

I want to know every word in the world
And I want to know its meaning.
I want to know how the pyramids were built
And why the Tower of Pisa is leaning.

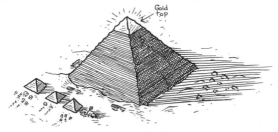

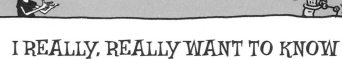

Write down four things that YOU really, really want to know. I've done the first one for you because I think we all want to know that.

FALSE FACTS

I REALLY, REALLY WANT TO KNOW

1. What is the biggest number in the world?

2.

3.

4.

5.

? ? ? ? ? ?

TROPHY TIME

Make a trophy for yourself. It could be for something you're good at (like eating the most pancakes at breakfast) or a talent you have (like being a good drawer or a fast runner), or simply for being you.

PET TROPHY TIME

What would you give your pet an award for (cuddliest, hungriest, noisiest)? If you don't have a pet, make a trophy for your favourite animal.

Draw your animal on the top of the trophy.

SPOT THE DIFFERENCE

SPOT THE DIFFERENCE

One of these pictures of Prince Potato is slightly different. Can you tell which one it is? Circle the number of the odd one out.

1

2

3

④

5

6

The answer is on page 163, but don't go there if you are not a vegetable because it's a Vegetables Only page!

TREEHOUSE ABC

Can you write in the missing words to finish this Treehouse ABC?

A is for

B is for

C is for

D is for

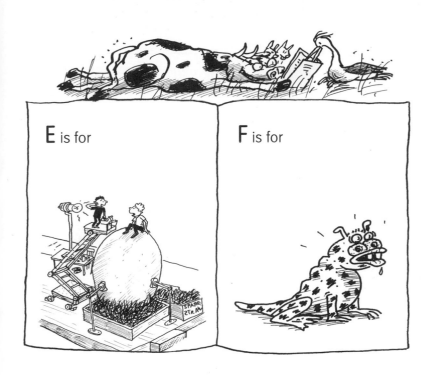

E is for

F is for

G is for

H is for

I is for

J is for

K is for

L is for

M is for

N is for

O is for

P is for

Q is for

R is for

S is for

T is for

U is for

V is for

W is for

X is for

Y is for

Yellow
↓

Z is for

Answers are on page 164.

LEARN TO READ WITH ... YOU!

See if you can make your own ABC. Can you think of a word for each letter of the alphabet that has something to do with you? Draw a picture too!

PIC OF YOU

This is a book
all about me,
the things that I like
and the things that I see.
It's my

YOUR NAME

ABC

E is for

F is for

G is for

H is for

I is for

J is for

KLUNK!

K is for

Llama!

L is for

M is for

N is for

O is for

P is for

Q is for

R is for

S is for

T is for

I eat carrots.

U is for

V is for

WUFF!

W is for

X is for

67

Y is for

Z is for

JILL'S HOUSE

This is a page from *The 13-Storey Treehouse* with some of the words missing. Can you write them in?

Jill lives on the other side of the forest in a house full of animals. She's got _two_ dogs, a goat, three _horses_, four gold _fish_, one cow, six _rabbits_, two guinea pigs, one _camel_, one donkey and one _cat_.

BAA!

SNAP!

MOO

Answers are on page 165.

PICTURE PUZZLE

 Write the name of each thing pictured on the opposite page into the grid below. Then read down the circled letters to discover the hidden word.

Write words across the grid.

The answer is on page 166.

1	(F)	i	r	e		
2	C	(r)	A	s	h	
3	S	P	(i)	d	e	r
4	T	U	b	(C)	M	e	n
5		C	l	o	(n)	E	S
6			h	a	N	(d)	S
7				A	n	t	(S)

1

2

3

4

5

6

7

COLOUR-BY-NUMBERS

Use the number guide to colour in the picture.

FINISH THE FACES

Can you finish drawing these faces for me, including mine?

How can he talk if he doesn't have a mouth?

Don't ask me—I can't hear you. I don't have any ears.

ANDY'S WORD SEARCH

When you've finished there should be 13 letters left over that spell out something to do with Andy.

WORD LIST

ANDRONICUS
ANDYLAND
AUTHOR
BOOK
CHIPS
CLONES
COMICS
FRIEND
NARRATOR
SANDWICH
SCRIBBLING
STORY
WRITING

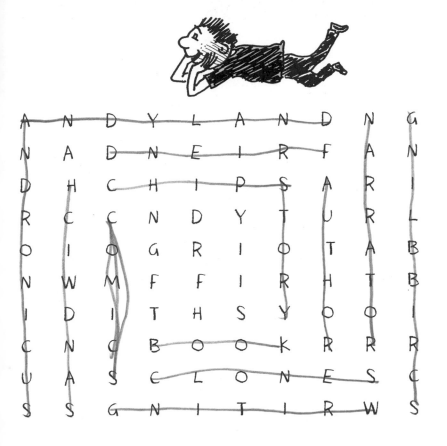

A	N	D	Y	L	A	N	D	N	G
N	A	D	N	E	I	R	F	A	N
D	H	C	H	I	P	S	A	R	I
R	C	C	N	D	Y	T	R	L	B
O	I	O	G	R	I	O	T	A	B
N	W	M	F	F	I	R	T	T	B
I	D	I	T	H	S	Y	O	O	I
C	N	C	B	O	O	K	R	R	R
U	A	S	C	L	O	N	E	S	C
S	S	G	N	I	T	I	R	W	S

SOLUTION: Andy Griffiths

Answers are on page 167.

75

SELF-INFLATING UNDERPANTS

Draw a picture of YOU wearing self-inflating underpants that have inflated just when you don't want them to.

TERRY'S WORD SEARCH

When you've finished there should be 11 letters left over that spell out something to do with Terry.

BARK

WORD LIST

Yikes!

BARKY
CLONES
DRAWING
FRIEND
ILLUSTRATE
INVENTIONS
MONKEYS
PENCIL
READ
STAR
TERENCIUS
TERRYTOWN
UNDERPANTS
YIKES

TERRY

ARGHHHHHHH!

78

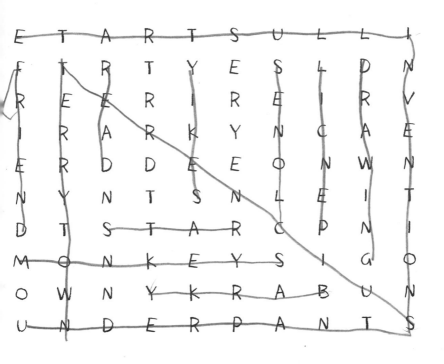

```
E T A R T S U L L I
F T R T Y E S L D N
R E E R I R E I R V
I R A R K Y N C A E
E R D D E E O N W N
N Y N T S N L E I T
D T S T A R C P N I
M O N K E Y S I G O
O W N Y K R A B U N
U N D E R P A N T S
```

SOLUTION: TERRY DENTON

Answers are on page 168.

TREEHOUSE CODE TIME

Use the Treehouse code to read my message.

B O O K S

a r c

F U N

The answer is on page 169.

I

L   O   V   E

YOU, THE READER

B   A   R   K   Y

BARK

Barky is saying the answer is on page 170.

Can you decode my message?

I know the answer. It's on page 171.

Can you figure out what the baby is saying?

G   O   O

G   O   O

 A   G   A

G   A   G   A

The answer is on page 172.

I know what I am saying, but do you?

I

K n o w

a L L

I know where the answer is. It's on page 173.

TATTOO TIME

JOKE TIME

Can you match each joke to its answer? Write the number of the joke next to its punchline.

JOKES

1. Where do cows go when their TV is not working?

2. Why couldn't the pirate play cards?

3. What bird is always out of breath?

4. How do monkeys make toast?

5. Where can you find out about spiders?

6. What do you call a sleeping dinosaur?

7. What is invisible and red?

8. What is a pirate's favourite letter?

9. Why was Cinderella kicked off the soccer team?

10. What do you get if you walk under a cow?

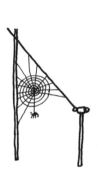

PUNCHLINES

 A. They put it under a gorilla

 B. The moovies

 C. Because he was sitting on the deck

 D. A puffin

 E. Because she kept running away from the ball

 F. Rrrrr

 G. A pat on the head

 H. A dinosnore

 I. On websites

 J. No tomato

> Answers on page 1,740,000. HA HA! Just joking! They are on page 174.

89

91-STOREY TREEHOUSE CROSSWORD

Use the clues to fill in the crossword.

ACROSS

1. Archways of colour you see in the sky (and sometimes coming out of noses).
3. Andy and Terry have this sort of island in their treehouse.
5. Where the giant spider lives.
7. Terry finds a medal for The World's Greatest
   — — .
8. The crazy land in the back of the wardrobe.
12. How many storeys Andy and Terry add to the treehouse each time.
13. How many wishes you usually get from a genie.

DOWN

2. The colour of the big button.
4. Andy saves everyone's life with his submarine
   — — — — — — — — .
6. What Mr Big Nose wants Andy and Terry to do for him.
9. The part of Mr Big Nose's body that explodes.
10. Madam Know- — — -all.
11. Madam — — — — -it-all.

1. Rainbows
2. R
3. desert 4. s 5. wel 6. B
7. D
8. Banarnia 9.
10. T 11. K
12. Thirteen
13. Three

Answers are on page 175. Goo-goo ga-ga.

CRYPTIC CLUES

Madam Know-it-all's cryptic clues are really hard. Can you figure out which treehouse level she is talking about?

I know you don't have time,
But I always do a rhyme.
So here's your cryptic clue
MARBAGE MUMP ... pee-uw!

The level is   *Garbage Domp*

If patting a baby dinosaur appeals to you,
Then go to the MAYBE WHINE-OH-SAW
BETTING BOO.

The level is   *Baby Dinosaur Petting Zoo*

If you want to shove something
sweet in your face,
Then the
MICE-SCREAM ZALA
is just the place.

The level is   Ice cream Parlour

If you want to bounce up as high as a jet,
Then try the BAMPOLEEN
(which doesn't have a net)!

The level is   Trampoleen

It's full of fools who all look the same,
And BERRYCLOWN is its name.

The level is   Jerry town

Answers are
on page 176.

DRAW BARKY

I love drawing pictures of Barky. Here's one I did of Barky at the beach.

You should draw a picture of Barky. Choose one of the settings below and draw a picture of Barky there.

AT THE MOVIES
AT THE FOOTY

AT THE PARK
AT SCHOOL

BARKY, THE BARKING DOG AT

STORIES AND STOREYS

Can you match the stories to the book? Write the number of storeys in the book title to show in which book the story happened.

1. Terry and I solve The Mystery of the Missing Mr Big Nose in The ___62___ Storey Treehouse.

2. Terry and I tell the story of Superfinger in The ___13___ Storey Treehouse.

3. Pirates take over the treehouse in The ___26___ Storey Treehouse.

4. Terry and I fly a dot-to-dot rocket to the moon in The ___39___ Storey Treehouse.

5. Spy cows spy on us in The ___72___ Storey Treehouse.

6. Terry and I travel through time in a wheelie bin in The ___68___ Storey Treehouse.

7. Terry and I babysit Mr Big Nose's grandchildren in The ___91___ Storey Treehouse.

FIND THE MATCHING PAIR

Circle the numbers of the two pictures of Vegetable Patty that are exactly the same.

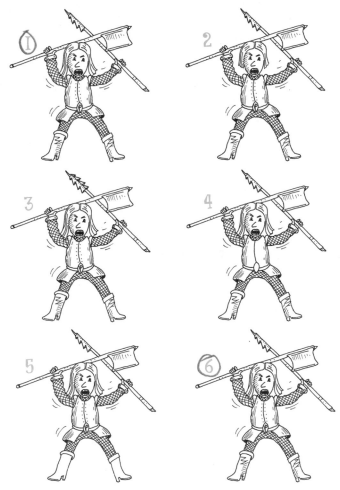

The answer is on page 177.

TREEHOUSE COLOUR IN

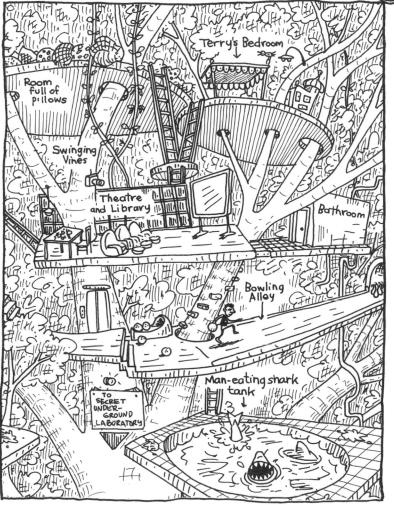

PICTURE PUZZLE

Write the name of each thing pictured on the opposite page into the grid below. Then read down the circled letters to discover the name of one of my favourite animals.

Write words across the grid.

The answer is on page 178.

1	(C)	O	W	S		
2	B	(A)	R	K	Y	
3	b	U	(T)	T	O	n
4	R	a	i	(n)	B	O	W
5		B	a	n	(a)	N	a
6			S	h	A	(R)	t
7				B	A	D	(Y)

1

2

3

4

5

6

7

HOME SWEET HOME

 Can you match the people and animals below with their homes on the opposite page?

You can live in a cottage.
A hutch or a nest.
An igloo is cool.
But a treehouse is best.

I

2

3

4

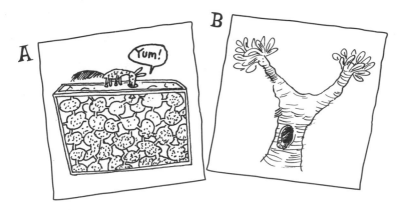

Write the correct letter next to each number.

1	C
2	A
3	D
4	B

The answer is on page 179.

SCRAMBLED ICE-CREAM

The labels on *Edward Scooperhands'* ice-cream tubs are all mixed up. Can you unscramble them and write the correct flavour under the tub?

COHOTEALC

choclate

ZAPZI

Pizza

NAVILLA

Vanilla

BERRYWARTS

Stranburry

TOH GOD

Hot dog

SHAGPETIT

Spagetti

MELONADE

Lemonade

VINSIBLIE

invisible

Flingy nomkey?!

FISHGOLD
PRISESUR

Goldfish
Surprise

FLINGY
NOMKEY

Flying
monkey

CROKY
DOAR

rocky road

DWINNIG
DOAR

winding road

Check page 180 to see if you got them right.

TRID DOAR

Dirt road

LELJY KANES

Jelly snakes

KASNES AND RADDLES

Snakes and ladders

MENKPOO

Pokemon

WACKY WAVING INFLATABLE ARM-FLAILING TUBE MEN FESTIVAL

In *The 91-Storey Treehouse* we waved our arms like a bunch of wacky waving inflatable arm-flailing tube men at a wacky waving inflatable arm-flailing tube men festival.

This is what an actual wacky waving inflatable arm-flailing tube men festival would look like. Colour it in and write what silly stuff the tube men might be saying in the speech bubbles.

WHERE ARE ANDY AND TERRY?
(Beginners)

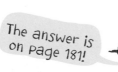

WHERE ARE ANDY AND TERRY?
(Intermediate)

Can you find the Andy that looks like this? And the Terry that looks like this?

The answer is on page 182!

WHERE ARE ANDY AND TERRY?
(Advanced)

Can you find Andy and Terry?

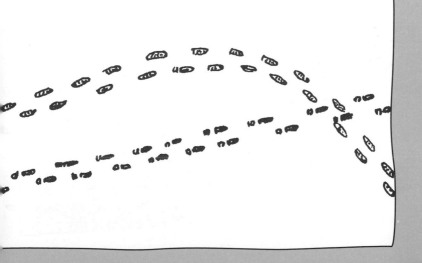

TREEHOUSE COUNTING FUN

 The pages in The Treehouse Counting Book are out of order and the numbers have fallen off. Can you write the numbers back in?

How many cows?

How many letters?

How many Andys?

How many horses?

How many penguins?

How many goldfish?

How many cats?

How many spiders?

How many snakes?

How many Ninja snails?

How many brussel sprouts?

How many guinea pigs?

How many rabbits?

Calm down, Andy, the answers are on page 183.

YOUR COUNTING BOOK

Make your own counting book. I've done the numbers: you do the drawings. You could draw things that are special to you, or they could be things from the treehouse.

1

2

3

7

8

9

10

122

11

12

13

WHO'S WHO?

 Do you know who all these characters are?

1. Who scoops the ice-cream?

2. Who delivers the mail to the treehouse?

3. Who is the world's greatest un-inventor?

4. Who is the world's greatest vegetable fighter?

Answers are on page 184.

5. Who directed the treehouse movie?

6. Who writes the words?

7. Who draws the pictures?

8. Who knows all and sees all?

9. Who publishes Andy and Terry's books?

KINGDOM COLOUR IN

Colour in the picture of my fantastic kingdom, Andyland.

ANT FARM COLOUR IN

Colour in the ant-packed action picture.

FIND THE BABY

Oh no! We've lost the baby!

Can you help us find it? It's somewhere in Jillville.

Great job, but, oops, we've lost it again.

 Yikes! Help us find the baby before Mr Big Nose realises it's missing.

 Answers are on page 185.

PICTURE PUZZLE

Write the name of each thing pictured on the opposite page into the grid below. Then read down the circled letters to discover the name of a Treehouse character.

Write words across the grid.

The answer is on page 186.

1	B	I	R	D		
2	S	I	L	K	Y	
3	L	I	G	h	t	S
4	P	l	a	n	E	t	S
5		S	C	O	O	P	S
6			H	O	R	S	e
7			H	O	S	e	

130

1

2

3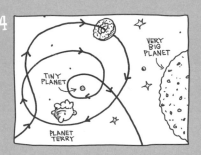

4

5

6

7

SPIN-AND-WIN FUN

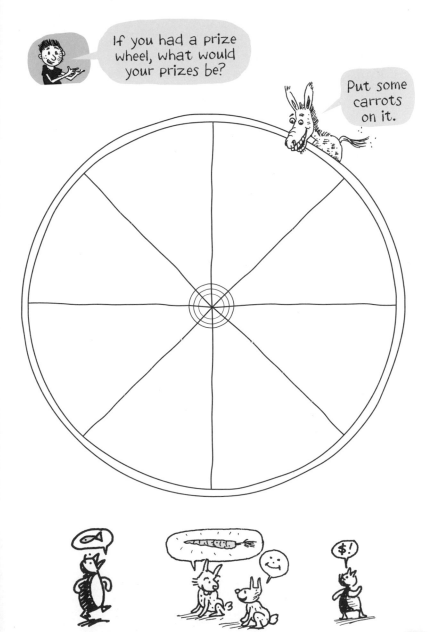

MULTIPLE CHOICE QUIZ

Tick the box that has the correct answer.

1. Mr Big Nose thinks Andy and Terry are qualified to be babysitters because:

☐ a) they act like babies

☐ b) they look like babies

☑ c) they worked in a monkey house

☐ d) they sleep like babies

2. Andyland is:

☐ a) the stupidest place on Earth

☐ b) the craziest place on Earth

☑ c) the Andyest place on Earth

☐ d) the rainiest place on Earth

3. Professor Stupido is:

☐ a) Andy's nickname for Terry

☑ b) an un-inventor

☐ c) a rap artist

☐ d) a history professor

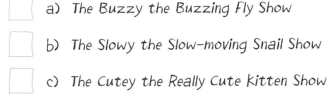

4. Terry's favourite TV show is:

☐ a) *The Buzzy the Buzzing Fly Show*

☐ b) *The Slowy the Slow-moving Snail Show*

☐ c) *The Cutey the Really Cute Kitten Show*

☑ d) *The Barky the Barking Dog Show*

Answers are on page 187.

THE MYSTERY OF THE MIXED-UP HATS

 Oh no. These characters don't look right at all. They're wearing the wrong hats.

Prince Potato

Grumpy Tomato

Inspector Bubblewrap

Detective Andy

Can you solve the mystery of the mixed-up hats by drawing a picture of what each character should be wearing on their head?

Prince Potato's
Crown

Grumpy Tomato's
Top Hat

Inspector
Bubblewrap's Helmet

Detective Andy's
Hat

 If you want to see if you solved the mystery, go to page 188.

CLOSE-UP FUN

I love looking at things through my magnifying glass, like this caterpillar ... and Andy.

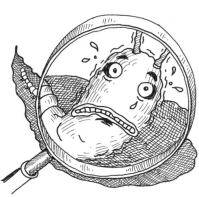

What would you like to see close-up? Draw it.

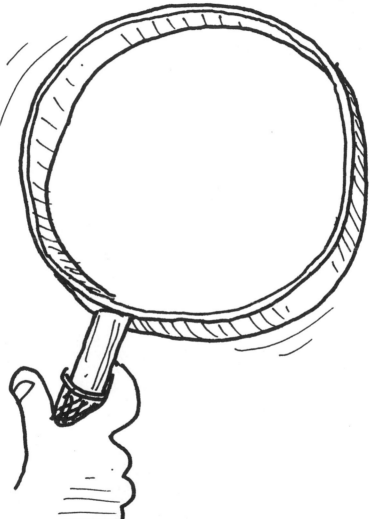

CHOOSE THE RIGHT WORD

It's easy to get words confused if they sound a bit alike. Can you tell which is the right one out of these pairs?

Tick the box to show which word is correct.

1. It swirls and sucks up people and houses.

☐ tomato   ☑ tornado

2. It's big and black and has eight legs.

☑ spider   ☐ spy cow

3. It spins around and is very powerful.

☑ whirlpool   ☐ girls' school

4. It drains people's brains.

☑ Turbanator   ☐ Trunkinator

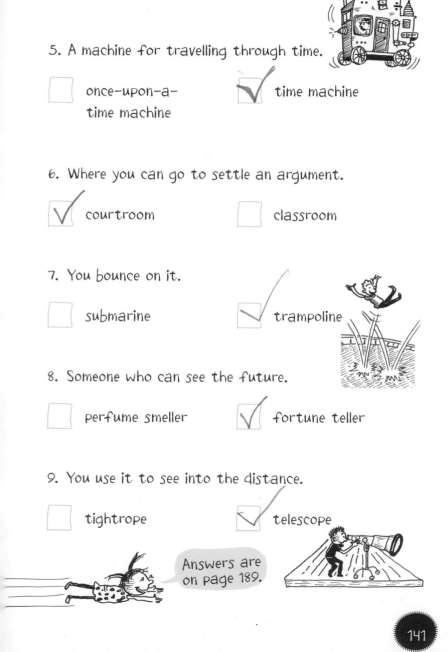

5. A machine for travelling through time.

☐ once-upon-a-time machine   ✓ time machine

6. Where you can go to settle an argument.

✓ courtroom   ☐ classroom

7. You bounce on it.

☐ submarine   ✓ trampoline

8. Someone who can see the future.

☐ perfume smeller   ✓ fortune teller

9. You use it to see into the distance.

☐ tightrope   ✓ telescope

Answers are on page 189.

THROUGH THE PORTAL

In *The 91-Storey Treehouse* Andy and I went through a portal into the crazy land of Banarnia.

If you could go through a magical portal, what type of place would you like to find on the other side? Draw it.

 Bottle World!

 Upside Down Land!

 Walking Car World!

Halfhorse-arnia!

PORTMANTEAU WORD FUN

Portmanteau words are words that are made by blending two other words together. Here are some examples.

spoon   +   **fork**   =   spork

spoon   +   pencil   =   spooncil

I invented that one!

Electric eel + unicorn
= electricorn! ZAP!

skirt   +   shorts   =   skort

breakfast   +   lunch   =   brunch

       Bok!
Bok!

chook   +   tortoise   =   chortoise

I invented that
one too!

Make up three portmanteau words by combining a word from Group A with a word from Group B. I've done one below, which you can draw.

No. You're a frogpotamus. But what am I?

Am I a portmanteau?

GROUP A		GROUP B
crab		rabbit
crocodile		trampoline
caterpillar		finger
snake		unicorn
foot	**+**	baby
nose		dinosaur
car		hippopotamus
bread		pencil
shoe		crayon
fairy		robot

PIC ⟶   PIC ⟶   PIC ⟶

crab + rabbit = crabbit

I'm a portmanteau. Cat + canary = catnary!

Yikes! Do you eat birds or seed?

GROUP A	GROUP B	PORTMANTEAU
	+	=
	+	=
	+	=

ANSWER TIME

WHO AM I? (PAGES 10–11)

Professor Stupido

Inspector Bubblewrap

Madam Know-it-all

Mel Gibbon

Mr Big Shot

Bill the postman

FILL IN THE BLANKS (PAGES 12–13)

Can you tell me the level?
Can you fill in the blank?
It's home to three fish—
It's the killer shark tank

If you don't like going
Around and around
Then stay off the
Not-very-merry-go-round

The person in charge
Is a bit of a clown
It's full of his clones
And it's called Terrytown

If you dare to go in
You will have entered your tomb
For there is no escape
From the treehouse Maze of Doom

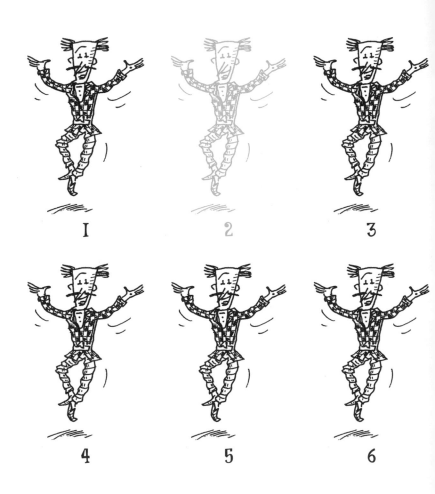

Number 2 is the answer:
Professor Stupido's moustache is missing.

TREEHOUSE TRUE OR FALSE? (PAGE 15)

T   F

1. Andy painted Silky yellow to make her a catnary.
   False: Terry did it.

2. Captain Woodenhead is a police captain.
   False: he's a pirate captain.

3. Terry is a really good drawer.

4. Andy is also a really good drawer.
   False: he's not. (No offence, Andy.)

5. Professor Stupido is an inventor.
   False: he's an un-inventor.

6. Terry is allergic to magic beans.

7. Mel Gibbon is a monkey.
   False: he's a gibbon (and he really hates being called a monkey).

8. Andy is very good at maths.
   False: he isn't.

9. Terry and Andy have a desert island level.

10. Mr Big Nose likes opera.

11. Vegetable Patty is a revenge-atarian.

12. I have an early learning centre for aliens.
    False: it's for animals.

13. Terry invented the spooncil.

Roses are red
Violets are blue
To solve a mystery
You need a clue

Roses are red
Violets are blue
You can pat a baby dinosaur
At the baby-dinosaur petting zoo

Roses are red
Violets are blue
Pets visit Jill's pet salon
When they want a new hairdo

Roses are red
Violets are blue
The number after one
Is the number two

Why Andy can't do maths.

C	O	W	S			P
A						I
R		S	T	A	R	R
R						A
O	W	L	S			T
T						E
S	H	A	R	K	S	

ACROSS

1 COWS: caterpillar, owls, watermelon, Silky

3 STAR: sign, tortoise, arrow, robot

4 OWLS: on/off switch, watermelon, llama, Superfinger

5 SHARKS: snake, hand, anteater, rhinoceros, knife, shark

DOWN

1 CARROTS: caterpillar, Andy, rabbit, rabbit, on/off switch, Terry, snake

2 PIRATES: penguins, ice-cream, robot, ant, tomato, Edward, shark

JILL'S NUMBER QUIZ (PAGES 20–22)

1. 13 storeys
2. 3 wise owls
3. 3 (2 children and 1 baby)
4. 10 unlucky pirates
5. 3 sharks
6. 78 ice-cream flavours
7. 1 grumpy old tomato
8. 100 years (and 15 minutes)
9. 13 flying cats (including Silky)
10. 78 plates
11. 1 punch
12. zero friends
13. 10 (10, 9, 8, 7, 6, 5, 4, 3, 2, 1, Blast off!)

91-STOREY TREEHOUSE WORD SEARCH (PAGES 28–29)

Solution: FORTUNE TELLER

FILL IN THE BLANKS (PAGES 30–31)

1. submarine **sandwich**
2. big red **button**
3. **garbage** dump
4. **tele**phone
5. **Bill the** postman
6. **crystal** ball
7. warning **poster**
8. Madam **know-it-all**
9. **spin-and-win prize** wheel
10. **emergency self-inflating** underpants
11. **Alice, Albert and the** baby
12. **Mr Big** Nose

DEFINITION QUIZ (PAGES 32–33)

TRUNKINATOR:
a boxing elephant

REVENGE-ATARIAN:
someone who eats vegetables to get revenge on them

PHARAOH:
an ancient Egyptian ruler

AUTOBIOGRAPHY:
a person's account of his or her own life

I should have played Andy in this puzzle. I would have been more convincing.

TERRY'S DRAWINGS SUDOKU (PAGE 37)

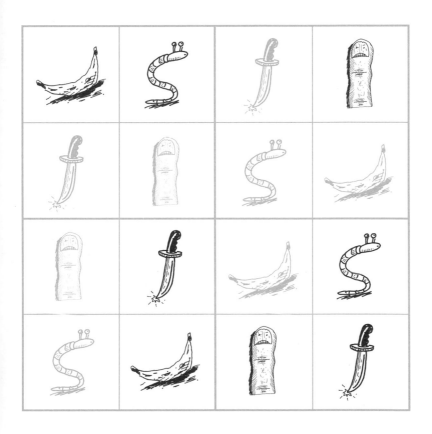

↓

O	L	G	I	O	R	O	S	S
D	P	N	B	H	C	E	R	E
E	X	O	Y	M	T	H	I	G
S	E	S	E	I	O	I	T	E
I	H	T	I	S	W	O	T	H
O	S	B	N	I	O	I	B	E
R	A	O	E	O	R	G	G	E
C	M	O	H	T	G	T	I	R

SHADOW PUZZLES (PAGES 44–45)

SPOT THE DIFFERENCE (PAGE 52)

Number 5 is different: Inspector Bubblewrap is not wearing a safety helmet. Yikes! That's not very safe!

SPOT THE DIFFERENCE (PAGE 53)

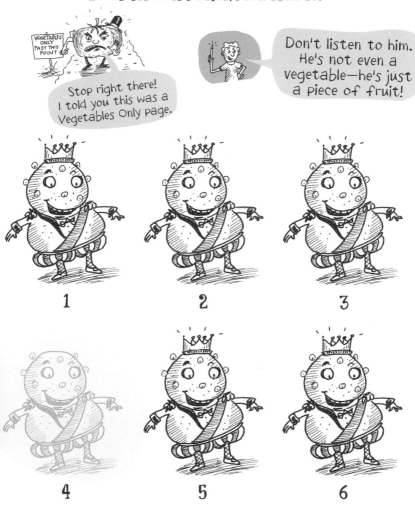

Number 4 is different: Prince Potato is not wearing his crown. He's no longer a prince—he's just a silly old potato.

TREEHOUSE ABC (PAGES 54–60)

A is for Andyland
B is for Birthday Card Bandits
C is for Cheeseland
D is for dinosaur
E is for egg
F is for frogpotamus
G is for gibbon
H is for hand
I is for ice skating
J is for Jill
K is for knife
L is for lights
M is for Maze of Doom
N is for nose
O is for Once-upon-a-time machine
P is for Prince Potato
Q is for quiz (or questions)
R is for rabbits
S is for Superfinger
T is for Trunkinator
U is for underpants
V is for Vegetable Patty
W is for waterfall
X is for x-ray
Y is for yellow
Z is for zoo

JILL'S HOUSE (PAGE 69)

Jill lives on the other side of the forest in a house full of animals. She's got two dogs, a goat, three horses, four goldfish, one cow, six rabbits, two guinea pigs, one camel, one donkey and one cat.

PICTURE PUZZLE (PAGES 70–71)

1	(F)	I	R	E		
2	C	(R)	A	S	H	
3	S	P	(I)	D	E	R
4	T	U	B	(E)	M	E	N
5		C	L	O	(N)	E	S
6			H	A	N	(D)	S
7				A	N	T	(S)

The hidden word is FRIENDS

ANDY'S WORD SEARCH (PAGES 74–75)

A	N	D	Y	L	A	N	D	N	G
N	A	D	N	E	I	R	F	A	N
D	H	C	H	I	P	S	A	R	I
R	C	C	N	D	Y	T	U	R	L
O	I	O	G	R	I	O	T	A	B
N	W	M	F	F	I	R	H	T	B
I	D	I	T	H	S	Y	O	O	I
C	N	C	B	O	O	K	R	R	R
U	A	S	C	L	O	N	E	S	C
S	S	G	N	I	T	I	R	W	S

Solution: ANDY GRIFFITHS

167

TERRY'S WORD SEARCH (PAGES 78–79)

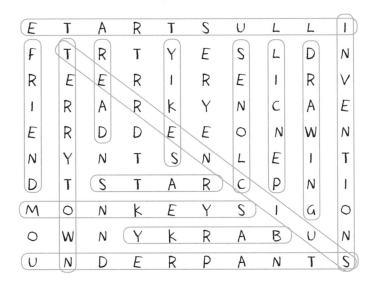

E	T	A	R	T	S	U	L	L	I
F	T	R	T	Y	E	S	L	D	N
R	E	E	R	I	R	E	I	R	V
I	R	A	R	K	Y	N	C	A	E
E	R	D	D	E	E	O	N	W	N
N	Y	N	T	S	N	L	E	I	T
D	T	S	T	A	R	C	P	N	I
M	O	N	K	E	Y	S	I	G	O
O	W	N	Y	K	R	A	B	U	N
U	N	D	E	R	P	A	N	T	S

Solution: TERRY DENTON

168

TREEHOUSE CODE TIME (PAGE 81)

Andy's message

B O O K S

A R E

F U N

TREEHOUSE CODE TIME (PAGE 82)

Terry's message

I

L   O   V   E

B   A   R   K   Y

TREEHOUSE CODE TIME (PAGE 83)

Jill's message

P   E   T   S

A   R   E

T   H   E

B   E   S   T

TREEHOUSE CODE TIME (PAGE 84)

The baby's message

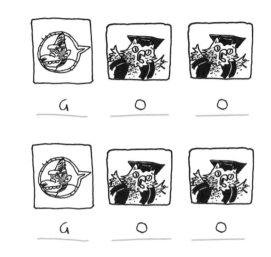

G   O   O

G   O   O

G   A   G   A

TREEHOUSE CODE TIME (PAGE 85)

Madam know-it-all's message

I

K   N   O   W

A   L   L

JOKE TIME (PAGES 88–89)

Ha ha, websites. That's funny!

1B Where do cows go when their TV is not working?
The moovies

2C Why couldn't the pirate play cards?
Because he was sitting on the deck

3D What bird is always out of breath?
A puffin

4A How do monkeys make toast?
They put it under a gorilla

5I Where can you find out about spiders?
On websites

6H What do you call a sleeping dinosaur?
A dinosnore

7J What is invisible and red?
No tomato

8F What is a pirate's favourite letter?
Rrrrr

9E Why was Cinderella kicked off the soccer team?
Because she kept running away from the ball

10G What do you get if you walk under a cow?
A pat on the head

R	A	I	N	B	O	W	S		
								R	
D	E	S	E	R	T		W	E	B
	A						D	A
B	A	N	A	R	N	I	A		B
	D			O					Y
I	W			S		K			S
T	H	I	R	T	E	E	N		I
	C					O			T
	T	H	R	E	E		W		

CRYPTIC CLUES (PAGES 92–93)

MARBAGE MUMP = garbage dump

MAYBE WHINE-OH-SAW BETTING BOO = baby-dinosaur petting zoo

MICE-SCREAM ZALA = ice-cream parlour

BAMPOLEEN = trampoline

BERRYCLOWN = Terrytown

STORIES AND STOREYS (PAGES 96–97)

1. Terry and I solve The Mystery of the Missing Mr Big Nose in *The 52-Storey Treehouse*.

2. Terry and I tell the story of Superfinger in *The 13-Storey Treehouse*.

3. Pirates take over the treehouse in *The 26-Storey Treehouse*.

4. Terry and I fly a dot-to-dot rocket to the moon in *The 39-Storey Treehouse*.

5. Spy cows spy on us in *The 78-Storey Treehouse*.

6. Terry and I travel through time in a wheelie bin in *The 65-Storey Treehouse*.

7. Terry and I babysit Mr Big Nose's grandchildren in *The 91-Storey Treehouse*.

FIND THE MATCHING PAIR (PAGE 98)

The matching pair is 1 and 6.

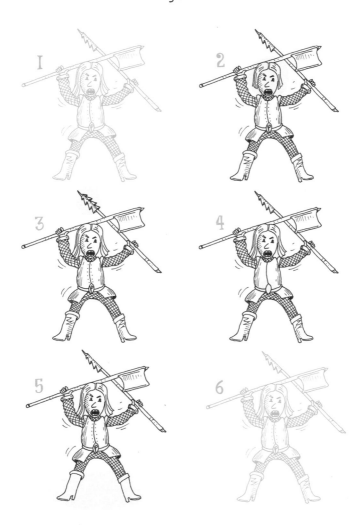

PICTURE PUZZLE (PAGE 100–101)

	1	2	3	4	5	6	7
1	(C)	O	W	S			
2	B	(A)	R	K	Y		
3	B	U	(T)	T	O	N	
4	R	A	I	(N)	B	O	W
5		B	A	N	(A)	N	A
6			S	H	A	(R)	K
7				B	A	B	(Y)

The solution is CATNARY
(one of my favourite animals).

178

HOME SWEET HOME (PAGES 102–103)

SCRAMBLED ICE-CREAM (PAGES 104–105)

 CHOCOLATE

 PIZZA

 HOT DOG

 SPAGHETTI

 VANILLA

 STRAWBERRY

 LEMONADE

 INVISIBLE

SCRAMBLED ICE-CREAM (PAGES 106–107)

 GOLDFISH SURPRISE

 FLYING MONKEY

 DIRT ROAD

 JELLY SNAKE

 ROCKY ROAD

 WINDING ROAD

 SNAKES AND LADDERS

 POKEMON

WHERE ARE ANDY AND TERRY? (Beginners)

(PAGE 110)

(PAGE 111)

WHERE'S ANDY AND TERRY? (Intermediate) (PAGES 112–113)

WHERE'S ANDY AND TERRY? (Advanced) (PAGES 114–115)

Solution: Andy and Terry are not here. They have left the picture.
(They have gone to get an ice-cream.)

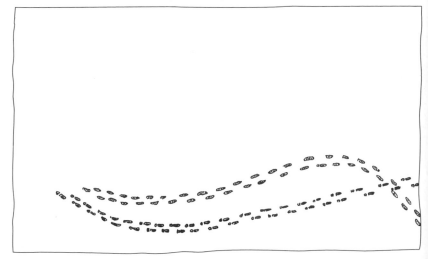

TREEHOUSE COUNTING FUN (PAGES 116–119)

one cow

two guinea pigs   three horses

four goldfish   five spiders

six letters   seven penguins

eight snakes   nine Ninja snails

ten Andys   eleven brussel sprouts

twelve cats   thirteen rabbits

WHO'S WHO? (PAGE 124–125)

1. Who scoops the ice-cream?
   Edward Scooperhands

2. Who delivers the mail to the treehouse?
   Bill the postman

3. Who is the world's greatest un-inventor?
   Professor Stupido

4. Who is the world's greatest vegetable fighter?
   Vegetable Patty

5. Who directed the treehouse movie?
   Mr Big Shot

6. Who writes the words?
   Andy

7. Who draws the pictures?
   Terry

8. Who knows all and sees all?
   Madam know-it-all

9. Who publishes Andy and Terry's books?
   Mr Big Nose

FIND THE BABY (PAGES 128–129)

I	(B)	I	R	D		
2	S	(I)	L	K	Y	
3	L	I	(G)	H	T	S
4	P	L	A	(N)	E	T	S
5		S	C	O	(O)	P	S
6			H	O	R	(S)	E
7				H	O	S	(E)

The name of the Treehouse character is BIG NOSE.

MULTIPLE CHOICE QUIZ (PAGES 134–135)

1. Mr Big Nose thinks Andy and Terry are qualified to be babysitters because:

   ☑ c) they worked in a monkey house

2. Andyland is:

   ☑ c) the Andyest place on Earth

3. Professor Stupido is:

   ☑ b) an un-inventor

4. Terry's favourite TV show is:

   ☑ d) The Barky the Barking Dog Show

WHEN TERRY AND I WORKED IN
THE MONKEY HOUSE.

THE MYSTERY OF THE MIXED-UP HATS

Prince Potato
wearing his crown

Grumpy tomato
wearing his top hat

Inspector Bubblewrap
wearing his safety helmet

Andy wearing
his detective hat

CHOOSE THE RIGHT WORD (PAGES 140–141)

1. It swirls and sucks up people and houses.
   - [ ] tomato
   - [✓] tornado

2. It's big and black and has eight legs.
   - [✓] spider
   - [ ] spy cow

3. It spins around and is very powerful.
   - [✓] whirlpool
   - [ ] girls' school

4. It drains people's brains.
   - [✓] Turbanator
   - [ ] Trunkinator

5. A machine for travelling through time.
   - [ ] once-upon-a-time machine
   - [✓] time machine

6. Where you can go to settle an argument.
   - [✓] courtroom
   - [ ] classroom

7. You bounce on it.
   - [ ] submarine
   - [✓] trampoline

8. Someone who can see the future.
   - [ ] perfume smeller
   - [✓] fortune teller

9. You use it to see into the distance.
   - [ ] tightrope
   - [✓] telescope

ALSO AVAILABLE

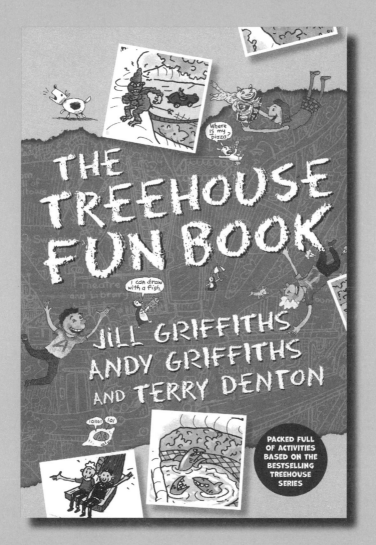

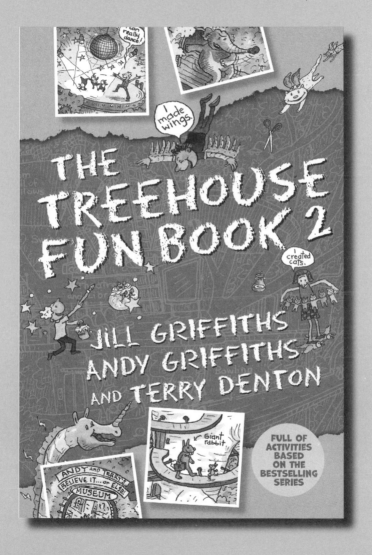

Lots of laughs

at every level!

Lots of laughs

at every level!